OLD BAG OF BONES
A Coyote Tale

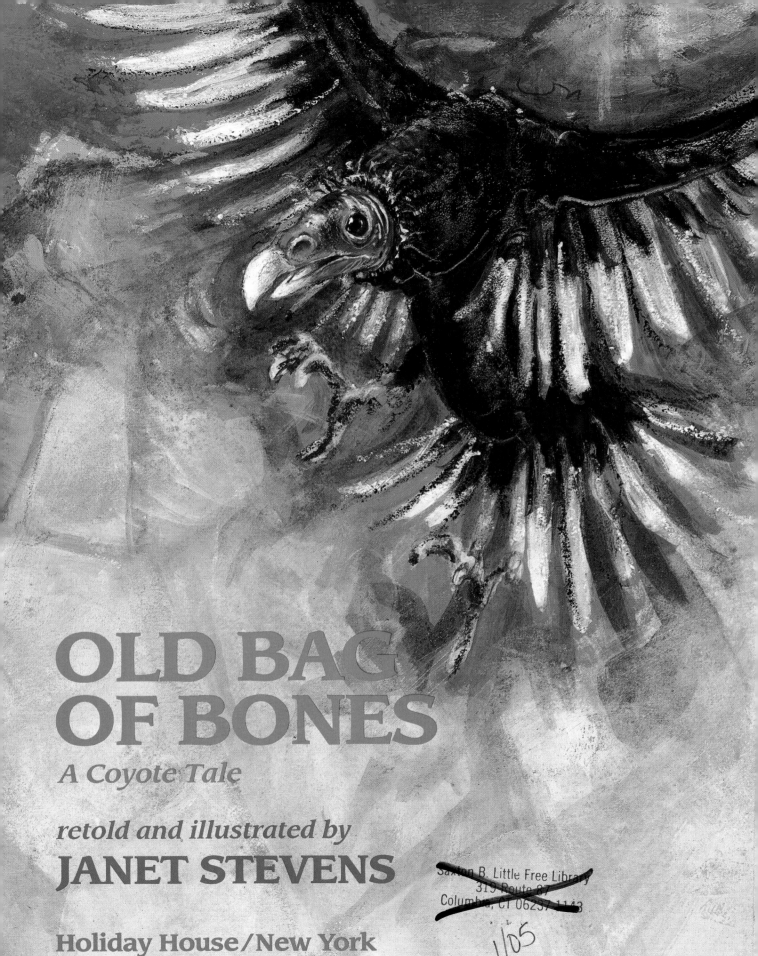

OLD BAG
OF BONES

A Coyote Tale

retold and illustrated by

JANET STEVENS

Holiday House/New York

Copyright © 1996 by Janet Stevens
ALL RIGHTS RESERVED
Printed in the United States of America
Library of Congress Cataloging-in-Publication Data
Stevens, Janet.
Old bag of bones : a coyote tale / retold and illustrated by Janet
Stevens. — 1st ed.
p.   cm.
ISBN 0-8234-1215-6 (hc : alk. paper)
1. Shoshoni Indians—Folklore.   2. Tales—Great Basin.   3. Coyote
(Legendary character)—Juvenile literature.   I. Title.
E99.S4S74   1996   95-31443   CIP
398.24′52974442—dc20
ISBN 0-8234-1337-3 (pbk.)

This tale is loosely based on "Old Man Coyote and Buffalo Power," a Shoshoni tale from
Plains Indian Mythology by Alice Marriott and Carol K. Rachlin, copyright © 1975 Alice Marriott
and Carol K. Rachlin, Thomas Y. Crowell Company, New York.

Old Coyote dragged himself to the top of the hill.

"Ohh," he groaned. "Look at me, I'm very old. I'm so old, I'm nothing but a bag of bones. I need food, but I can't see it, and if I can't see it, I can't catch it. Even if I did catch it, I couldn't chew it because I don't have any teeth. So here I sit, an old bag of bones. I'm just going to lie down and die. Good-bye, world!"

Buzzard flew above Coyote. "Ten, nine, eight, seven, six, five . . . You're almost dead," screeched Buzzard.

"Go away, I'm not gone yet," said Coyote. "Just leave me alone to rest in peace. Come back when it's finally over," grunted Coyote.

"Wow, Coyote, look down the canyon at Young Buffalo. Isn't he something?" asked Buzzard.

"I can't see that far!" complained Coyote.

"I'll describe him to you. He's big, young, and strong. I know he has special powers."

"Oh," said Coyote. "Do you think Young Buffalo could share some of his strength, youth, and power with me? He provides food, shelter, and clothing for the people, so why couldn't he help me? I think it's worth a try. Go away, Buzzard, I'm not your dinner yet."

New hope surged through Coyote as he limped down the hill.

"Hello, Young Buffalo," said Coyote. "You certainly are big, powerful, young, and strong while I'm just an old bag of bones. Do you think you could spare a little youth? A drop of strength? And a touch of power would be nice, too."

"What?" Young Buffalo snorted. "You must be kidding, you old trickster!"

"No, I'm not. Please! You are my only hope. I'm on my last legs, and Buzzard is waiting for me to die."

"You *are* in sorry shape," said Young Buffalo. "Oh, I guess it can't hurt to help you out. I will give you strength and youth, but no power. Only a true young buffalo has power. Now, follow me to Bear Butte."

When they arrived, Young Buffalo said, "Close your eyes, Old One. You're about to be changed forever." He charged and circled Old Coyote. He snorted and puffed and kicked up dust. Coyote coughed, AAGH-AAGH, and sneezed, ACHOO. The fourth time around, Young Buffalo rammed into Old Coyote.

They both tumbled down Bear Butte . . .

and landed with a crash.

When the dust cleared, Young Buffalo said, "Open your eyes, Coyote."

Coyote looked at himself. He had changed into a young buffalo!

"Yippee," he snorted, "I'm young again."

"That's right," said Buffalo. "But remember, Coyote, even though most of you looks like a young buffalo on the outside, on the inside you are still a powerless coyote. See, I left your coyote tail to remind you. You are a coyotalo! Or maybe a buffote. Let's call you that—a buff-OH-tee. Don't forget that a buffote has no power or you'll get into trouble. Now, be off with you!"

Buffote strutted around in his new skin. He ran to the water hole and looked at his reflection.

"Look how handsome I am!" he remarked to himself. "Anyone who looks this strong and youthful must have power."

Old Rabbit limped over to the water hole for a drink.

"Hey, Old Rabbit, look at me! I'm young and strong. Look at you, you're a pitiful sight," said Buffote.

"I don't mind being old," said Rabbit. "Age brings wisdom."

"What? You like being old? How silly, Old Rabbit."

Forgetting Young Buffalo's warning, Buffote blurted out, "I can make you young like me. I'm powerful as well as young and strong."

"Sounds tricky," said Rabbit.

"No, no, no! Trust me. I have the power to make you young again!"

At that, Buffote butted Rabbit high in the air. He landed on Buffote's back.

"I'll give you a ride to Bear Butte. It won't take long, and I'll change your life forever."

Not far down the path, they ran into Old Wrinkly Lizard.
"What a pathetic thing you are, Old Lizard. Your days are
numbered," said Buffote.

"I may look old, but I've got some good years left," said the lizard. "Age brings respect. I'm great-great-grandfather to a whole pack of lizards, and they respect me," explained Lizard.

"You're kidding." Buffote laughed. "They couldn't care less about you, Old Wrinkly One. They have their own lives to live and will leave you alone to die. You better come with us."

He picked up Old Wrinkly Lizard by his tail and swung him onto his back. "I'll make you young again, and you will thank me for it!"

The group had almost reached Bear Butte when a mangy kangaroo rat stumbled by.

"Out of the way, Old Rat. See that buzzard, he's just waiting for you."

"Not so," snapped Old Kangaroo Rat, "there's plenty of life left in me."

"Ha," said Buffote. "Youth is everything."

"No, it's not," said Old Kangaroo Rat. "Age brings experience. I have done many things and seen many places. I am rich with experience."

"Hogwash," said Buffote. He grabbed Old Kangaroo Rat by the leg and flung him on his back with the others.

"I'll make you young, and you will be happy."

Finally, they arrived at Bear Butte. Buffote lowered his head and the animals slid off. He began marching and prancing around the group.

"Close your eyes, Old Ones," Buffote ordered. "You're about to be changed forever."

Buffote charged and circled the animals. He snorted and puffed and kicked up dust. The old ones coughed, AAGH-AAGH, and sneezed, ACHOO. The fourth time around, Buffote rammed into them.

They all tumbled down Bear Butte . . .

and landed with a crash.

When the dust cleared, Rabbit opened his eyes, Lizard opened his eyes, and Kangaroo Rat opened his eyes. They looked at each other.

"We look the same as before, just a little dustier," cried Rabbit.

They began searching for Young Buffalo. There was no buffalo anywhere. All they saw was one straggly, dusty, old coyote, an old bag of bones.

"My goodness," declared Kangaroo Rat. "It was just Old Coyote in a buffalo suit. We should have known."

"How silly!" remarked Lizard. "Old Coyote is even wrinklier than I am. Let's get out of here."

The three old animals dusted themselves off and hobbled down the path.

"Oh, phooey!" moaned Coyote. "I'm back where I started, old as ever." He struggled to the top of Bear Butte. "There's that buzzard again. Get out of here! I hate being old. It was such fun prancing around with all that energy."

Buzzard's stomach growled. "Four, three, two . . ." he said.

"Stop, Buzzard," said Coyote. "Look, isn't that another young buffalo darting across the valley? It looks like he is riding a horse."

"You can't see anything," said Buzzard. "That's not a young buffalo! That's someone wearing a young buffalo hide."

"Oh my, young buffalos don't last long," remarked Coyote. "Hmmm, maybe being an old coyote isn't so bad after all. Shoo, Old Buzzard. I bet I have some grandchildren somewhere. I'm going to find them, so they can value my wisdom, respect me, and hear of my rich experiences. Maybe they'll give me dinner."

While Old Coyote hobbled down the path in search of his family, a majestic elk caught his eye. Coyote was overwhelmed by his youth and energy. Without a moment's hesitation he howled out, "Hello there, Young Elk. You certainly are big, powerful, young, and strong. How about sharing some of your power with an old bag of bones like me?"